POPCORN

* A *

FRANK ASCH
Bear Story

Parents' Magazine Press * New York

E

Library of Congress Cataloging in Publication Data

Asch, Frank.
  Popcorn.
  SUMMARY: Sam Bear invites his friends to an
impromptu Halloween party and asks them to bring a treat.
  [1. Popcorn—Fiction   2. Bears—Fiction.
3. Halloween—Fiction]   I. Title.
PZ7.A778Po 1979   [E]   79–216
ISBN 0–8193–1001–8
ISBN 0–8193–1002–6 lib. bdg.

To Mark Alan Stamaty

One fall night,
Mama and Papa Bear
went to a Halloween party,
and left Sam home alone . . .

...so he called up his friends
and invited them to his house
for his own Halloween party.

While he waited
for his friends to arrive,
he made himself a costume.

The first to arrive was Betty.
"I brought some popcorn
for the party," she said.

The second to arrive was Billy.
He brought popcorn, too.

Bernie, Bonny, and Buster
also brought popcorn.

In fact, everyone brought popcorn!

The party was lots of fun.

When Betty said,
"Hey, let's pop all that popcorn,"
everyone thought it was a good idea.

With some help from his friends,
Sam lifted Mama Bear's great big
kettle onto the kitchen stove
and poured in all the popcorn.

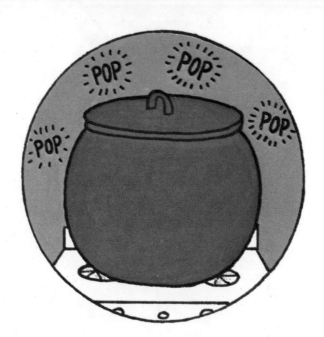

He added some oil and salt
and turned on the stove.
Soon it began to pop. POP! POP! POP!

There was so much popcorn,
it quickly filled the kettle
and spilled out onto the floor.

There was so much popcorn,

it filled the whole kitchen.

It spilled out into the living room.

It filled all the rooms downstairs
and crept upstairs.

There was
so much popcorn,
it filled
the whole house.

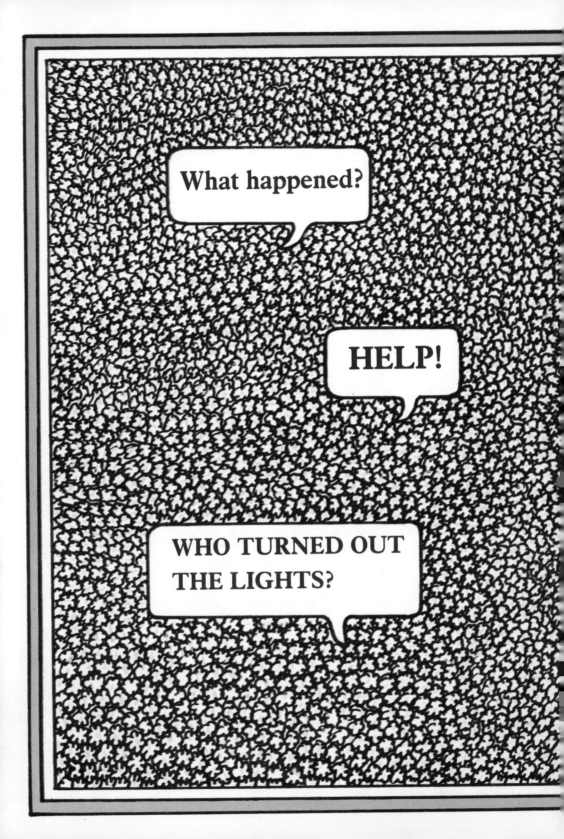

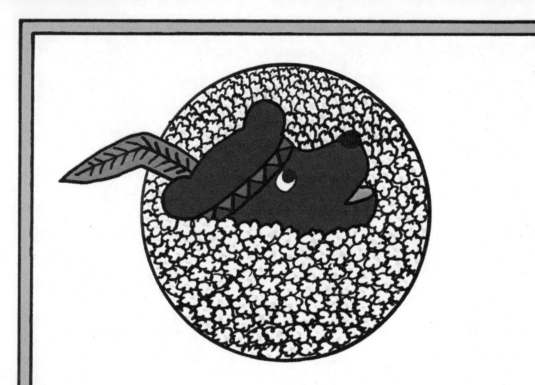

Everyone wanted to go home,
but Sam said, "No, you've
got to stay and help me
get rid of all this popcorn,
or I'll be in big trouble."

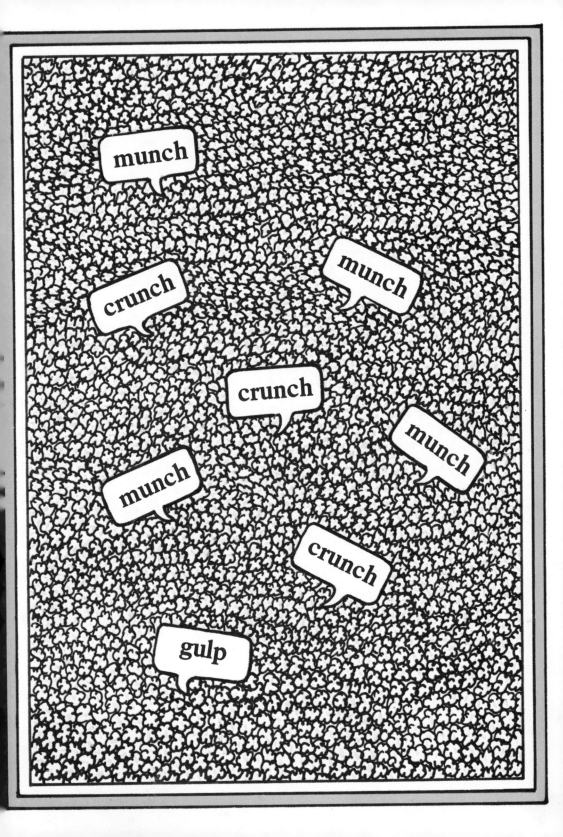

They ate and ate and ate . . .

and ate and ate and ate...

and ate and ate and ate...

until all the popcorn was gone.

"I don't care if I ever see
another piece of popcorn
in my whole life," said Buster.

"I feel like my stomach
is going to burst," said Betty.
"Mine, too," said Bobby.

Sam felt the sickest of all.
He said good night
to his friends,
and cleaned up....

and went to bed.

Later that night,
Mama and Papa Bear came home.

"Wake up," they said.
"We brought you a present."

"What is it?" asked Sam.

"Popcorn!" they replied.

About the author/artist

Frank Asch is the award-winning author/artist of several picture books. Among them are two earlier books for Parents': *Monkey Face* and the Bear Story *Sand Cake*. He and his wife, Janani, live in Brooklyn, Connecticut.